Where's the Starfish?

BARROUX

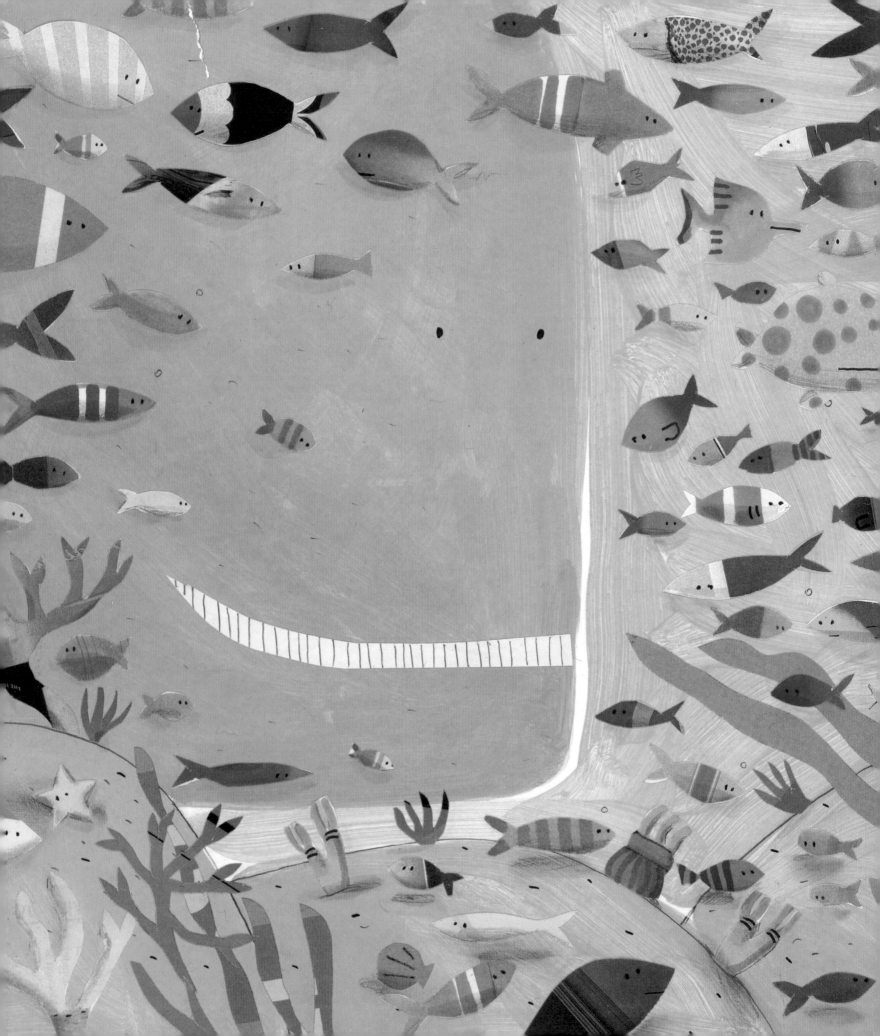

Where's the Starfish?

Where's the Jellyfish?

Where's the **Clownfish?**

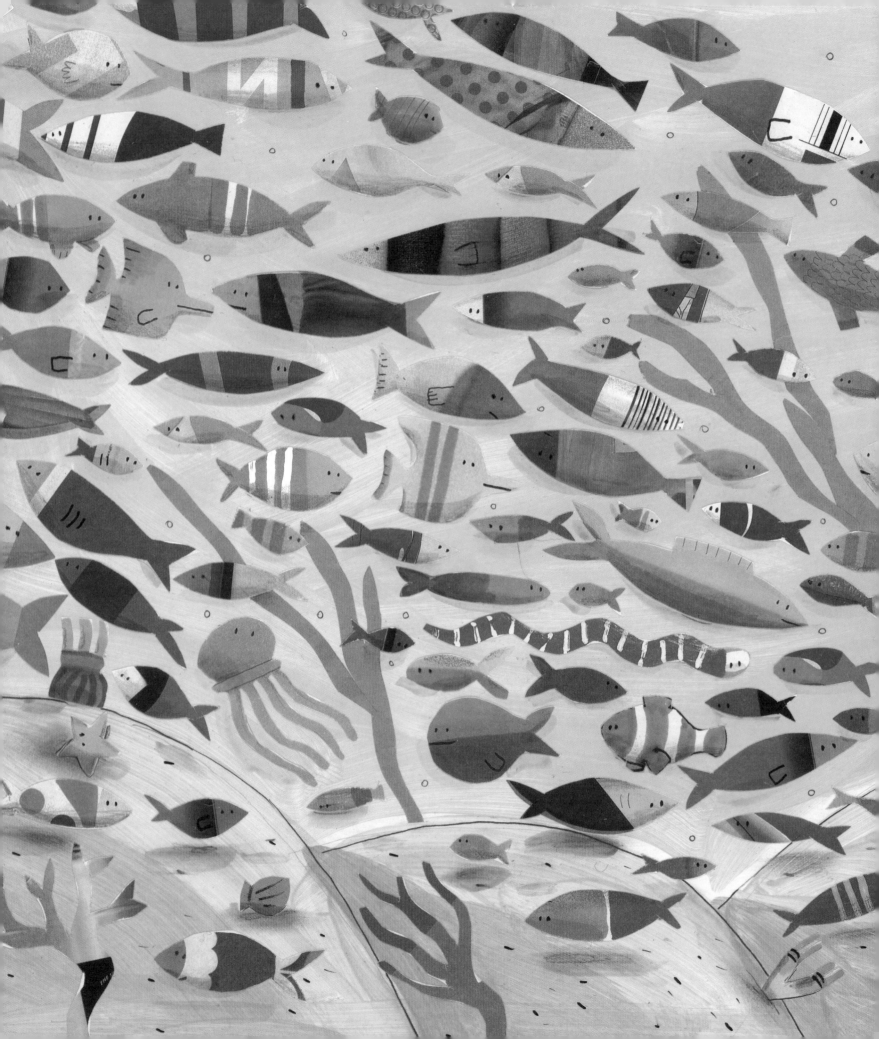

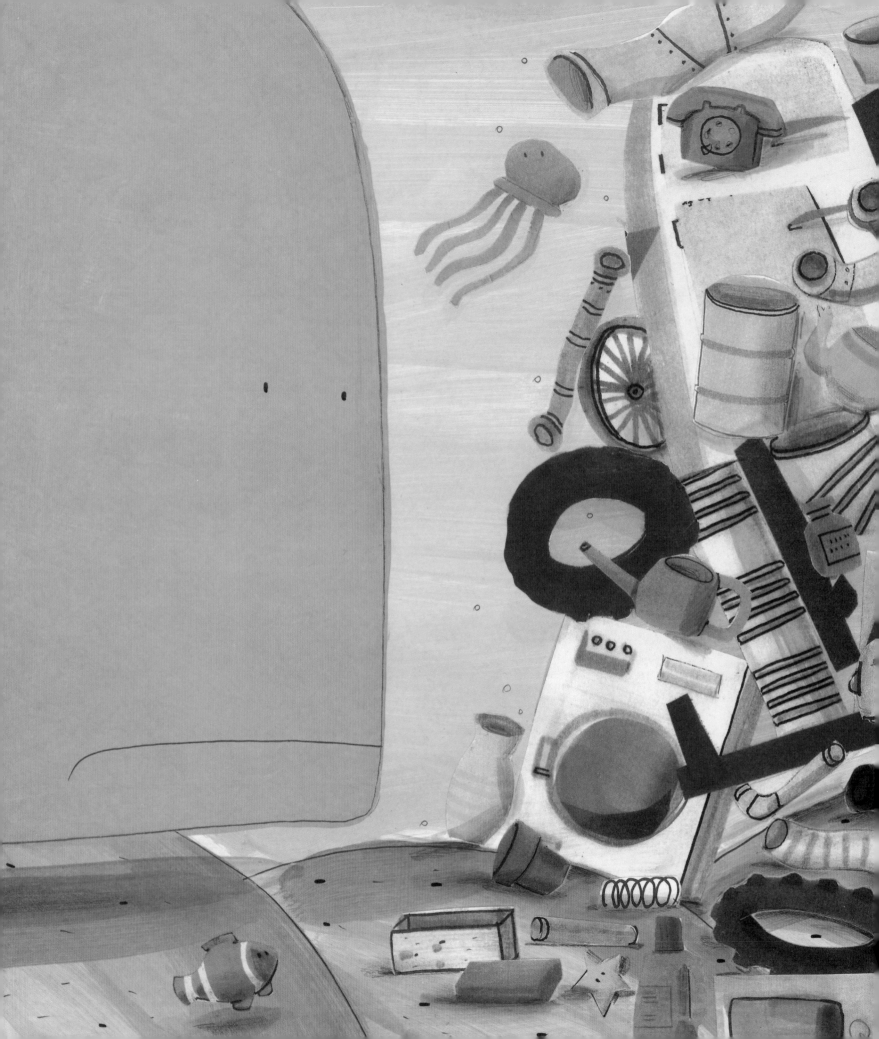

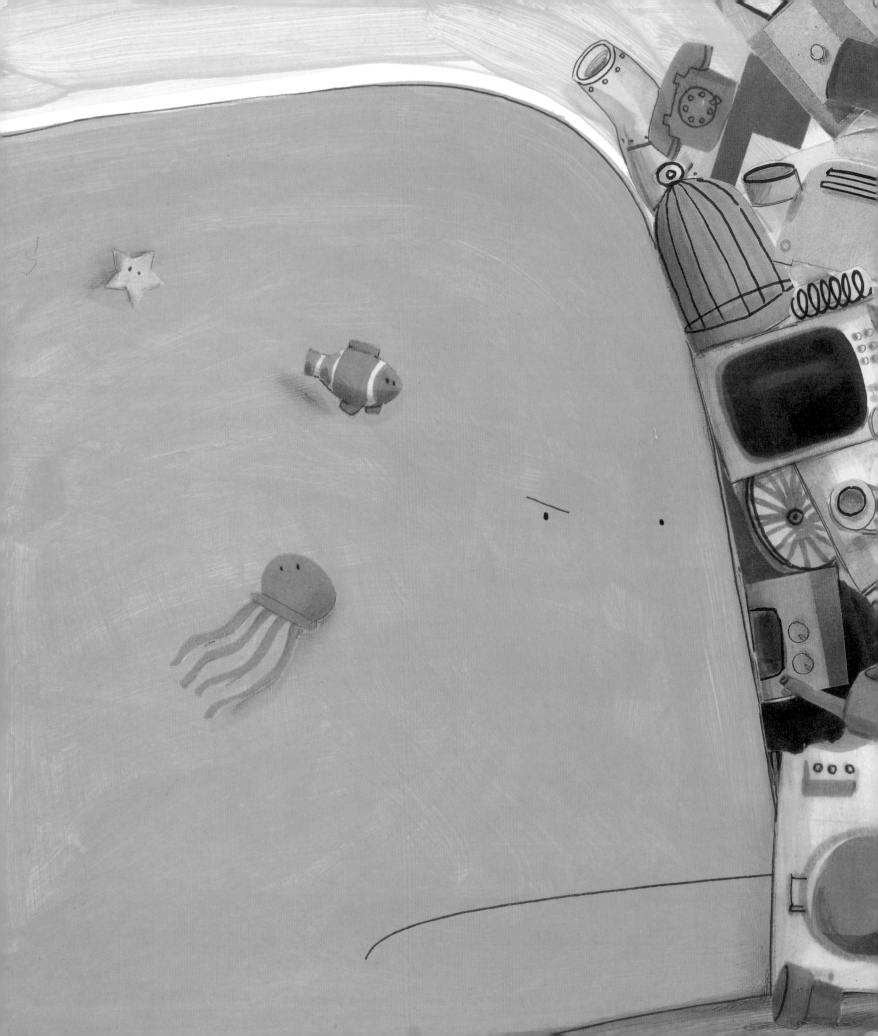

THE STORY BEHIND THIS BOOK

While on holiday, I saw a plastic bag that looked like a jellyfish and it inspired me to write a book about the threat of pollution to our waterways and oceans. We must protect these important underwater kingdoms for the creatures that live in them, and everyone needs to remember to take litter home and put it in the bin!

BARROUX

To Marguerite, Annabelle and Milan

FSC
www.fsc.org
MIX
Paper from
responsible sources
FSC® C018306

EGMONT
We bring stories to life

First published in Great Britain 2016
by Egmont UK Limited
The Yellow Building, 1 Nicholas Road, London W11 4AN
www.egmont.co.uk

Text and illustrations copyright © Barroux 2016
Barroux has asserted his moral rights.

ISBN 978 1 4052 8008 2 (hardback)
ISBN 978 1 4052 7139 4 (paperback)

A CIP catalogue record for this book is available from the British Library.